SCREAMS IN SPACE

Raintree is an imprint of Capstone Global Library Limited, a company incorporated in England and Wales having its registered office at 264 Banbury Road, Oxford, OX2 7DY – Registered company number: 6695582

www.raintree.co.uk
myorders@raintree.co.uk

Original illustrations © Capstone Global Library Limited 2020
Originated by Capstone Global Library Ltd
Printed and bound in India

ISBN 978 1 4747 7201 3
23 22 21 20 19
10 9 8 7 6 5 4 3 2 1

British Library Cataloguing in Publication Data
A full catalogue record for this book is available from the British Library.

SCREAMS IN SPACE

THE FINAL MISSION

BY STEVE BREZENOFF
ILLUSTRATED BY JUAN CALLE

raintree
a Capstone company — publishers for children

INTO THE DARK . . .

When you look up at the night sky, do you ever wonder if scary, creepy, horrible things happen up there just as they do on Earth? Sounds can't travel through outer space because there's no air. So if frightened people were out there, we'd never even hear their screams . . .

The spaceship *Meddler* travels the galaxies looking for valuable scrap to sell. The captain's daughter, Amelia, is never allowed to join in the dangerous work. But when she and Greeny, a dog-boy from another planet, team up and disobey orders, they soon find themselves facing brutal aliens in what might be their *Final Mission*.

The *Meddler* seemed to float impossibly. It was large and heavy-looking, and it was shaped more like a giant steel brick than a sleek spaceship. Its crew was a group of pirates and adventurers. And they filled the *Meddler*'s cargo bay with their prize: collected scrap.

That's what the crew of the *Meddler* did. They travelled from star system to star system. Along the way they gathered bits of metal, pieces of old technology and whatever other valuable materials they could find. Then they sold them.

Usually the scrap came from dead spaceships that orbited dead planets or dying stars. These were damaged ships whose crews had been gone for a long time. Or the crew was still on board but unable to make the repairs needed to keep travelling.

The dead ships had suffered accidents, or they'd run out of fuel or they'd blown a gasket. Or sometimes the *Meddler* blew a gasket for them. The *Meddler* wasn't above piracy, and it put them on the wrong side of the law across the galaxy.

The *Meddler*'s captain liked it that way. It added to the adventure and the ship's reputation.

Amelia Lightheart, twelve years old and the youngest member of the *Meddler*'s crew, squirmed on her stool in the officers' mess hall. The captain sat on the other side of the table and sipped steaming black coffee from a dented metal cup.

The captain of the *Meddler* was known by most of the crew as Fist. The nickname had been earned over years of leading the crew. The *Meddler* never met a law officer its captain couldn't fight off, often one-on-one and with fists flying.

Fist kept one eye on Amelia. The other was hidden behind a gleaming metal eye patch. "We're taking him on as cabin boy," Fist said in a gruff voice. It meant, *Don't argue with me.*

"Mum," Amelia said. For Fist was, in fact, Captain Jessamine Lightheart – Amelia's mother. "Greeny is *impossible.* Couldn't you just get a dog instead?"

"Amelia," said Fist. "I asked you not to bring up D-O-Gs when we're talking about Greeny."

After all, Greeny didn't look like an average boy. He looked like a human mixed with a white terrier. He came from a small planet called Canus.

The *Meddler*'s last stop had been at two of Canus' moons. They had fought tooth-and-nail with local security guards. But the guards weren't trained to deal with a whole ship of pirates, and the moons were on the edge of Canus' system. The guards didn't have time to call in help from the Canus Anti-Piracy Police Force.

The *Meddler* crew was lucky. The CAPF were known as the fiercest and cruellest officers in the solar system. They were willing to do anything to protect the property of Canus.

That was why the captain had chosen to strike the planet's two outer moons. Her crew was in and out before the CAPF had a chance to attack.

It was a good thing. Amelia hadn't gone on the mission, but she had seen the security videos. She'd had a look at the moons' guards.

The Canus people were like huge wolves. Their long snouts opened to reveal rows of sharp, yellow teeth. Their narrow eyes were rimmed in red. Their huge paws held ragged claws that could cut a person to shreds as well as hold a blaster.

The security guards were poorly trained, and yet they had fought furiously. Amelia didn't want to think about what it would've been like to battle the skilled and brutal CAPF.

But thanks to Captain Fist's quick wits, the *Meddler* escaped the moons with no losses and one of the largest scores they'd ever taken. And one furry little stowaway.

He called himself Greeny. The boy was nowhere near as scary as the adults of Canus. Greeny was more like a puppy than a bloodthirsty wolf. When they had found him hiding in the launch bay, he'd said he was looking for adventure.

Right then Amelia had known her mum would let him stay on the ship. Greeny was leaving home to find his place in the galaxy, just like Jessamine Lightheart had done when she was a girl. The dog-boy spoke the captain's language.

Of course, Amelia felt the same way. She wanted excitement and adventure. She wanted to find her own path. But Mum never seemed to notice that.

"Morning!" Greeny said as he pushed through the swinging metal door. He sniffed the air. "I smelled that bacon from bed and just had to get some."

"Oh, *please* join us," Amelia said. Her voice dripped with sarcasm as much as her pancakes were dripping with maple-flavoured syrup.

The officers' mess hall was usually off-limits to the crew. Only the captain, her daughter and the first mate were allowed to eat there.

But apparently Greeny wasn't quite up on the rules yet. Or he was a bit too slow to understand them completely. Or maybe he just didn't care.

Greeny used his hairy paws to scoop up five slices of bacon from the steel worktop. Then he hopped onto the chair next to Amelia.

"*Mmm*," he said. He shoved a whole strip of bacon into his mouth. "Oh, and it's not too crispy. Perfect."

"Greeny," Fist said, standing. She glanced at Amelia.

"Mum, please," Amelia said in a whisper.

With his mouth full of slightly chewy bacon, Greeny turned towards the captain. His big, brown, puppy-dog eyes grew even wider.

"Aye, Captain?" Greeny said.

Amelia saw bacon fat shoot from his mouth.

"You've been aboard for a few days now,"
Fist said.

Greeny nodded, his tongue hanging out of the
side of his open mouth. Obviously his mind was
still on the bacon.

"And for the most part," Captain Fist went on,
"you've been a good addition to the crew."

"Ha!" Amelia said.

Her mother gave her an icy, Captain Fist glare.

"If you're still interested in staying aboard,"
the captain said to Greeny, "I believe I can offer
you a permanent position."

"Really?" Greeny said, excited. "You won't
make me go back to Canus?" He snatched another
piece of bacon and shoved it into his mouth.

"Really," the captain said with a small smile.

"And you don't mind that I stowed away?" Greeny asked. His ears drooped in worry.

"Let's face it," Captain Fist said with a shrug. "That's how most of the crew got their start in this business, including myself."

"Not to mention the *Meddler* is wanted on Canus for piracy," Amelia muttered. "So heading back there is out of the question. Unless we want to be captured by the Canus Anti-Piracy Police Force and rot away in a prison cell for the rest of our lives."

Captain Fist shushed her. She put a hand on Greeny's shoulder. "And you like it here, right?"

"Of course," Greeny replied. "I love it."

"Then I hereby offer you membership on the crew of the *Meddler*," Captain Fist said.

"YES!" Greeny shouted. It was more like a bark, actually. "What will my rank be? Can I be your first mate?"

Amelia rolled her eyes.

"Well . . . ," Fist said, "that role is already taken. But I think we'll start you at cabin boy. You'll keep doing what you've been doing since we found you on board: sweeping up, running errands, doing chores . . ."

Greeny sagged a bit. "Oh," he said.

"You can always work your way up to other responsibilities," the captain said. "It'll just take time. You've only been with us a few days."

"And you smell funny," Amelia said. "If I were the captain, I'd drop you off at the nearest gas giant and be done with you."

"Amelia!" Captain Fist said.

Amelia crossed her arms. "It's what pirates *do*, Mum," she said. "We're heartless outlaws."

"Well, not *this* pirate," Captain Fist said. She turned to Greeny. "Now, Cabin Boy Greeny, how about you pick up the dishes as your first order."

The communications speaker over the table crackled and whined.

"Captain," said Sen, the first mate, over the comm. "Long-range scanners are picking up a major debris field around a planet. It's three hours to starboard."

The *Meddler* crew always talked about distances in units of time. All Captain Fist wanted to know was how long it would take to reach the next score.

Captain Fist pressed the black button on the table to turn on her mic. "What minerals are in the field?" She released the button.

"Scanning now," Sen said. After a few minutes, he reported, "Iron . . . eighty per cent. Carbon . . . eighteen per cent. Traces of . . . gold, platinum and zinc."

"That sounds like it could be a fleet of wrecked ships," Amelia said. "Are we going to move on it?"

Her mum raised one finger as she pushed the black button again. "Any activity?"

"Negative, Cap," Sen replied. "The debris field is dead quiet."

Captain Fist tapped her chin thoughtfully. Amelia held her breath.

The captain nodded. "Set a course," she said into the mic. "On my way to the bridge."

"Yes!" Amelia said. She hurried after the captain. Greeny began to follow.

"Whoa, whoa, Cabin Boy," Amelia said, spinning to face him. "You have your orders, remember? Clear those dishes, wipe the table and clean the worktop. Then *maybe* you can ask for permission to come onto the bridge. Got it?"

Greeny's hairy brow furrowed into a deep, angry V. "Don't talk to me like that, Little Fist," he snarled. "You're not my captain."

Amelia flinched, surprised by Greeny's sudden anger. For a moment, he had looked like a growling wolf. She recovered as best she could and backed out of the mess hall.

"Whatever," she said. "Just tidy up."

The *Meddler* reached the debris field's system in just three hours. First Mate Sen's travel estimates were almost never wrong. The only time Amelia remembered him being off was because Space Police had boarded for a surprise inspection.

Captain Fist had managed to get out of that one with no arrests and no fights. It was a miracle. Amelia's mum was great under pressure.

"What's on the long-range scans?" Fist said. She walked back and forth in front of her captain's chair. She almost never sat down in it.

Although they were in the right star system, the debris field was still millions of kilometres away. The *Meddler* couldn't risk getting any closer. The huge ship might bring unwanted attention from galactic law enforcement.

"Same as before, Captain," said Dr Pectin, the science officer. She repeated the elemental figures.

"All right," Fist said. "Whose turn is it?"

The *Meddler* itself was far too large to move through a debris field. So for most jobs, two crew members went out on a fast spaceship called the *Saber*. It was small, but it could make the journey on its own and easily gather scrap. The *Meddler* would stay close enough to communicate with the *Saber*, but no closer.

Sen pulled the tablet computer from his hip and poked the screen a few times. "Last crew out was . . . myself and Jerrette," he reported.

"That puts Yaz and McCarthy up for this mission," Fist said. She went to her chair and pressed a button on the arm. "Yaz and McCarthy to the *Saber*," she said, and her voice echoed through every speaker on the ship. "Move it."

"Mum," Amelia said.

The captain didn't look at her. Instead she took a deep breath and let it out through her teeth.

"Captain," her mother whispered. "When we are on the bridge, it's *Captain*."

"Sorry," Amelia said. "Captain."

"What is it, Ensign?" her mother replied, but she still didn't look at her.

"Captain Fist," Amelia said. She threw her shoulders back and stood as tall as she could. "I believe it is *my* turn to go on a mission. *I* am next on the list."

Her mother finally looked over. "Amelia," she said in a quiet voice.

"Ensign," Amelia corrected her. "When I turned twelve, you said you'd add me to the list of crew who get to go on missions. You put my name last, but I kept my mouth shut. It took eight months for my turn to come up, but now it has."

"I know," her mother said. She sat down in the captain's chair. "I know what I said, but . . ."

The speakers crackled. A voice came through. "Yaz and McCarthy on the *Saber*, Captain," the voice said. "Ready to launch on your say-so."

"Captain," Amelia said. "Please."

Her mother looked in her eyes.

Amelia's heart thumped against her chest. She had wanted to go on a mission since she was a little girl. But she was also terrified.

Captain Fist pressed a fingertip onto the mic button. "Go ahead with the final checks, Yaz and McCarthy," she said. "You have permission to launch when ready."

"Aye, Captain," Yaz replied.

"Mum!" Amelia said. She could feel the eyes of the bridge crew on her as tears ran down her cheeks.

"I'm not ready to send you out there yet," her mother whispered.

"*You* were out there at my age," Amelia shouted. She didn't care what the bridge crew thought of her.

"Yes, I was, and I know how dangerous it is," the captain said.

"Dangerous?" Amelia said. "It's a load of dead ships and scrap! What can happen?"

"Anything can happen!" said Captain Fist. She slammed her hand down hard on the chair's control panel.

Amelia jumped.

"Scans aren't perfect, Little Fist," the captain went on. "What if one of those 'dead ships' still has a crew? An *armed* crew?"

"I–" Amelia started. "I don't know."

"I do," the captain said. "I know. Because *I've* been a twelve-year-old girl trying to collect whatever scrap I could find. I barely stayed alive. I could count on one hand the number of times I went onto a dead ship and nothing went wrong."

Amelia let her mother's words settle for a moment before she replied. "But one of the junior officers would be with me," she said as calmly as she could manage. "They could handle any–"

"That's enough, Amelia," her mother said. She put her head in one hand.

"But, Mum–" Amelia protested.

"I said that will do, Ensign Lightheart!" Captain Fist snapped. "Go to your quarters, and stay there till mess call."

Amelia knew better than to keep arguing at that point. "Aye, Captain," she said, her voice small and quiet.

Amelia lay on the narrow bed in her quarters. Unlike most of the crew, she had a private room. It had been one of her mother's better attempts at making Amelia happy aboard the *Meddler*. The room was small, but it was hers.

There came a tapping sound on the metal door. "Knock, knock," a voice said. It was Greeny.

"Go away!" Amelia said. "I'm sleeping."

"You're talking," Greeny called through the door. "That means you're not sleeping."

Amelia sat up. "So? What do you want?" she snapped.

The door slid open, and Greeny sprang into the room.

"I thought that door was locked," Amelia said, lying back down again.

"I heard what happened on the bridge," Greeny said. He dropped to the floor and sat on the rug with his legs crossed. Greeny almost never sat in chairs or slept in his bed. He preferred the floor.

"How did you hear?" Amelia asked. It wasn't like the bridge officers reported everything to Greeny.

"Why does it matter?" Greeny said. His eyes twinkled playfully. "The point is you want to check out the debris field, and so do I."

"You?" Amelia said. She lifted her head to hit him with a glare. "Why should you get to go? You're just a cabin boy."

"I can help you get onto the *Saber*," Greeny said. "Which means I get to come too."

Sneak aboard the Saber? Amelia thought. The captain would kill her. Or worse, take away the little rank she'd actually earned aboard the *Meddler*.

"Mum gave the OK for them to leave thirty minutes ago," Amelia pointed out. "The *Saber* is probably already at the debris field."

Greeny shook his head, his tongue wobbling back and forth. "Yaz had to make some repairs. A part in the thrusters needed to be replaced," he said happily. "They won't launch for another fifteen minutes or so, I bet."

Amelia was almost disappointed to hear that. If the *Saber* had already left, she wouldn't have to choose whether to disobey the captain's direct order. But now . . .

"Come on, Little Fist," Greeny said. "You know as well as I do that the captain isn't going to let you go on a mission to gather scrap for *years*, if ever."

Amelia sat up and crossed her arms. "She might," she said. "I'm on the list."

"And we saw today how much that helps," Greeny said.

Amelia turned her back on Greeny. She stared out of her porthole into the outer edge of yet another star system. In the distance, she could just make out a dwarf-star sun. It was barely a dot.

"Where are we, anyway?" she asked.

"Pakvilde System," Greeny said quickly.
"I think. So are you in, or what? If we're going
to do this, we have to move now."

Amelia turned towards him. She put on as
confident a face as she could manage. "All right,
Cabin Boy. I'll go," she said. "But remember,
I outrank you. That means I'm in charge."

"Of course, Ensign," Greeny said, jumping
to his feet. He saluted. "If you'll follow me?"

With that, Greeny hurried out of the door as
it slid open. He practically galloped along the
corridor. Amelia had to run to keep up.

"Where are you going?" she called when
Greeny turned off the main corridor. He was going
away from the launching bay.

Greeny didn't answer. He just grinned back at
her, showing his fangy teeth. "This way," he said.

Greeny ducked under a railing and knelt next to the wall. He started removing screws from a metal grate. His sharp claws were perfect for the job.

Amelia watched the fur-covered boy work. "I can't believe we're doing this," she said.

"Relax," Greeny said. "No one ever comes down this corridor. Besides, I've done this loads of times."

"You've sneaked into the air vent system? Why?" Amelia asked.

Greeny pulled the grate off the wall. "It's the best way to get around the ship."

"You could just use the corridors," Amelia said.

"Put it this way," Greeny said. "If I hadn't been in the air vents, I wouldn't know about your disappointing morning on the bridge."

Amelia let that info sink in for a moment. She imagined the layout of the bridge. "That grate right under the security panel," she said, "right behind Mum's chair. You were in there?"

Greeny nodded, grinning. "You go first. I'll pull the panel back on from inside."

Amelia's second thoughts and doubts fired in her brain like a blaster battle. But she pushed them aside. She climbed into the vent. It was chilly inside – and cramped.

"Are you sure this is OK?" she asked. "Like, you're sure it's safe? It feels so . . ."

"Scary?" Greeny finished. "My people love tight spaces like this. But I know you humans from Earth One sometimes panic in them."

"Oh, so you're an expert in humans now?" Amelia said as she crawled through the tube. She came to a split. "Which way, left or right?"

"Left," Greeny said. "And no, I'm no expert. But I talk to the humans down in engineering. They hate climbing into the air system. They call the fear of small, closed-off spaces claustrophobia. I love the vents, though. I'd be in here all the time if I could."

"Anyway, I'm not even a human from Earth One," Amelia said. "I was born on the *Meddler*, so I'm a human from the *Meddler*. From space."

"Huh," Greeny said. "That's an interesting way to look at it."

"What's that supposed to mean?" Amelia said.

"Nothing at all," Greeny said. "Better pick up the pace."

Amelia groaned, but she crawled faster. Ahead, she could see slivers of light. It was the lights of the launch bay coming up through a grate.

"We're here. I see the launch bay," she said. "How do I get the grate off?"

"Let me slip around you," Greeny replied.

Without giving her any time to reply, Greeny pushed past from behind. Amelia was pressed to one side in the cramped tube.

"Ow!" Amelia cried. Some of Greeny's long nails sunk down into her hand. "Watch what you're doing! Those claws hurt."

"They're supposed to," Greeny said. "We're a fierce people, you know."

He flexed his claws. Then he got to work on unscrewing the grate from the inside.

"If you love your people so much," Amelia said, "why did you leave Canus and stow away on the *Meddler*?"

A flash of anger crossed Greeny's face. But as quickly as it came, it was gone. Amelia wasn't even sure if it had been there at all.

Greeny laughed. "You know why I left. For the same reason you're here, doing this," he said. "Because we both want adventure. We want to see what this galaxy is like outside of our tiny little lives. Mine back at home, and yours here on the *Meddler*."

Gently, Greeny tapped off the corners of the grate. Then he turned it sideways and pulled it into the tube without making a sound. "OK, I've got it."

In the room below sat the *Saber*. The ship was only big enough to carry a few people on short trips. It had nowhere near the range of the *Meddler*. But in many ways, Amelia liked the *Saber* better.

The ship was sleek and built to move quickly through nearly any atmosphere, or none at all. Its hull, though dented and scratched, was painted a wicked-looking orange and black.

Below, Amelia could see Yaz lying underneath the *Saber*. She was working on the thrusters. Her blowtorch made a lot of noise.

McCarthy leaned against the *Saber*'s hull nearby. He was looking lazily at the e-pad in his hand.

At the rear of the ship, the entryway was open and the walkway was out.

"Now is our chance," Amelia said. "Yaz is busy, and McCarthy never looks up from a screen unless something blows up."

Greeny grinned and dropped down from the open grate. His bare feet hit the floor silently.

Amelia jumped after him, crouching as she hit the metal floor. It still hurt, though.

Staying low, Greeny hurried around the side of the *Saber*. As Amelia had guessed, McCarthy didn't even look up. And Yaz, of course, couldn't hear or see anything while she worked on the thrusters. The smell of the blowtorch even covered up Greeny's stink.

Amelia and Greeny came to a stop at the *Saber*'s open entryway. "Now what?" Amelia said.

"Now," Greeny said, "you take over. I've never been on the *Saber*."

Amelia groaned in frustration. She looked around. Straight ahead was the ship's command bridge. There was a large front window and various control panels and technical displays. Along the walls were storage lockers that held important equipment for the mission.

There wouldn't be room in the storage lockers to hide. Amelia looked down and smiled.

"There," she said.

"Are we gonna crawl through more air vents?" Greeny asked.

Amelia shook her head. "It's the cargo bay, or what Mum calls the basement," she said. "It's where they'll put large pieces of scrap. Ship parts that still work, computer hardware, tanks of fuel – stuff like that."

Amelia crept further into the ship. She knelt down and opened a hatch in the floor.

"Won't they be able to find us in there?" Greeny asked.

"Maybe," Amelia said. She sat on the edge of the hatch. "But by then it'll be too late to put us back on the *Meddler*. Come on."

Amelia lowered herself down, and Greeny jumped in after. He gave her a boost, and she closed the hatch.

Inside the basement, it was completely dark.

Amelia pulled an e-pad from her hip and turned on the display. Its gentle blue glow filled the large storage area.

Greeny's face, lit from beneath, looked oddly sinister. When he opened his mouth in a smile, his sharp teeth seemed more threatening than friendly.

"Are you sure it's safe down here?" Greeny said. "There aren't any seat belts – or seats, for that matter."

"Sure I'm sure," Amelia said. "There are straps along the walls for tying down cargo. We can hold on to those. We'll be fine."

Suddenly Greeny's toothy grin looked more panicked. Amelia could hardly believe she'd ever seen Greeny's puppyish face as anything other than curious, and a little afraid.

The sound of footsteps pounded on the metallic floor over their heads. The ramp glided in, and the door closed with a *thwack*.

Yaz's voice on the comm came into the cargo bay. It was muffled, though. The kids couldn't make out what she was saying. But it soon became clear.

The *Saber*'s thrusters roared to life. Amelia and Greeny could hear the *Meddler*'s launch bay doors open, scraping and squeaking. It was loud enough to wake the dead.

Greeny whined from deep in his throat. He panted gently. His smell became even worse.

"Don't be scared," Amelia said. She put her e-pad on the floor and scooted to the younger crew member's side. "We're on an adventure, remember?"

Greeny nodded, his tongue hanging from his open mouth.

Amelia put an arm around his shoulders and pulled him gently. "Let's move to the wall," she said.

Greeny nodded again. Amelia scooped up her e-pad and hurried over. Just as she reached the wall, the *Saber* rumbled. It was lifting off.

She grabbed hold of a strap along the wall and helped Greeny grab one too. A fraction of a second later, the *Saber* blasted out of the *Meddler* and into open space.

There was almost no light. A warning lamp above the cargo door cast a dim, eerie red glow over the whole basement.

Amelia and Greeny sat in silence. Not that they could've talked much over the roar of the thrusters.

After thirty minutes, the *Saber* slowed and stopped. The thrusters went quiet. Their sound was replaced by the gentle hum of the ship's hover engines.

"We're here," Amelia whispered. With the thrusters off, she imagined Yaz and McCarthy right over their heads and able to hear everything she said.

She heard boots on the floor above. For several minutes, the two crew members shuffled around.

A loud beeping began. The ship's robotic voice announced, "Prepare to depressurize. Depressurizing now."

There was a loud hiss as air was let out of the air lock. Amelia could picture Yaz and McCarthy in their suits, standing in the sealed room. Before they left the *Saber*, the air needed to be pumped out of the air lock. If they tried to leave without depressurizing, all the air in the ship would rush out into space. And it'd happen so fast that it'd blast everything else out of the ship too.

The hissing slowed. Then, silence.

"They're gone," Amelia told Greeny. "They've started the spacewalk to gather scrap. It should be OK to leave the basement."

With a boost from Greeny, Amelia stepped into the main part of the *Saber*. The bridge was empty.

"Come on up!" Amelia called. She reached into the darkness. Greeny's furry hand took hers, and she pulled him onto the bridge.

"You're very light," Amelia said.

Greeny snarled. "I'm getting bigger."

Amelia and Greeny went over to the controls. The lights on the panels shined gently. Yaz and McCarthy had put the ship in hover mode while they worked. Through the cockpit window, Amelia saw the *Saber*'s crew moving among the debris field.

Amelia could see at once that the debris here was from a fleet of old ships. Panels of metal and fibreglass, many in good condition, drifted by. They moved slowly around a large, orange planet.

There were electrical parts too. None of that biotech stuff that was used in all the new ships. Nearby, Amelia saw a navigation panel and a dented comm dish. They could sell those pieces for a good price.

Glass and thick plastic shards floated in the debris field as well. They weren't worth anything, but they sparkled like glitter in the ugly wreckage.

And a single piece could also tear a hole in a spacesuit.

Be careful out there, you two, Amelia thought. The crew was like her family.

"All right," Amelia said. She looked down at the control panels. "I'm going to signal Yaz."

"Won't she be angry?" Greeny asked.

"Probably," Amelia admitted. She picked up the comm mouthpiece from the panel. "*Saber* to Officer Yaz, do you read?"

The speakers crackled. "Little Fist?" Yaz said. "Is that you?"

"Hi, Yaz," Amelia said. She almost laughed. "Greeny and I are aboard the *Saber*."

The figure outside the ship turned her helmeted head towards the cockpit window. "I see you," Yaz said. She sighed. "The captain is going to kill you. And me."

"And me," McCarthy added over the comm. "How are you doing, Little Fist?"

"Fine," Amelia said. "Sorry, guys. We couldn't help ourselves. Besides, the captain was never going to *let* me go on a mission."

Yaz sighed again. She was easily frustrated, but Amelia knew she loved her. Yaz had been like a big sister to Amelia her whole life.

"All right," Yaz said. "No fixing it now. Just sit tight while we gather the scrap. And since you're there, make yourself useful. Open the cargo bay's exterior doors, all right?"

"Will do," Amelia said. She clicked off the comm and nodded to Greeny. "Hit the blue panel on the end, next to the nav chair."

"Here?" Greeny said. He sat in the navigator's seat. There, a small panel glowed pale blue with different characters and symbols.

Greeny looked back at Amelia. "Which one? I can't read."

"Tap the big square in the centre," Amelia said.

Greeny did. The panel turned red and beeped.

A loud hiss came from below. Then a deep hum that Amelia could feel in the pit of her stomach. She was glad they had come up to the bridge before the basement opened. She didn't want to be sucked into space without any protection.

"The cargo bay is depressurizing," Amelia said. "When the panel is green, tap the square again."

The hum stopped. The hissing grew quieter and then silent. Greeny hit the green panel. They could hear the doors beneath slide open.

"Get comfortable in there," Yaz said over the comm. "There's a – wait. What was that?"

"What was what?" Amelia said.

McCarthy replied, "I saw it too. Investigating. Hold on."

A few moments later, Yaz's voice came on again. "Report, McCarthy."

McCarthy didn't reply.

"Ensign Lightheart," Yaz said.

Amelia gulped. That was her rank and surname. Something serious was going on.

"Aye, Officer Yaz?" Amelia replied.

"Any life readings on the bio scanner . . . aside from me?" Yaz asked.

"Checking now," Amelia said. She pressed a few buttons on the panel.

With help from Yaz, Amelia had spent the last year studying everything about the *Meddler* and the *Saber*. She had wanted to be prepared for her first mission – and to show her mum how serious she was. Amelia felt thankful she knew enough about the *Saber* to be useful.

The results came on the screen.

"I see McCarthy," Amelia said. "He's on the far side of a large chunk of eighty per cent iron and ten per cent aluminum and ten per cent—"

"OK, Little Fist," Yaz said. "That's fine. What's McCarthy's status?"

Greeny hunched next to Amelia. She heard and felt his breath on her ear, and she shivered.

"He's alive," Amelia said. "But his pulse is low. Body temperature is dropping. I think he's in shock or unconscious."

"Understood," Yaz replied. "I'm going to try to reach him. Stand by."

Amelia and Greeny watched through the window. Outside, Yaz used the thrusters on her pack to move through the field of debris.

The panel beeped. Amelia gasped.

"Officer Yaz," Amelia said. "I have an alert on the bio scan."

"Is McCarthy's condition worse?" Yaz asked.

"Negative, he's fine," Amelia said. "But I have two . . . no, three more life readings."

"Repeat, Lightheart?" Yaz said. "Three other life readings?"

"Affirmative, Yaz," Amelia said. "I see three life readings out there with you. They're surrounding McCarthy. Be careful."

"*AHH!*" Yaz screamed. The channel clicked off.

"Officer Yaz, come in!" Amelia shouted. "Officer Yaz!"

There was no reply.

"Yaz?" Amelia tried again. "Please answer me."

Still, radio silence.

"Yaz," Amelia said, her voice breaking in her throat. "Where are you?"

"There," Greeny said. He pointed at the bio scan panel with one long-nailed, hairy finger.

Yaz's blue dot glowed on the screen. It was close to McCarthy's. The three white dots – the unknown life forms – moved quickly towards it.

Suddenly the blue dots blinked off. Only the white dots remained.

Amelia felt cold. It was as if all the blood in her body had rushed to her feet and drained into the metal floor.

"W-we have to contact the *Meddler*," Greeny said. His voice shook. "They can help us."

Amelia didn't reply straight away. She thought while she slowed her breathing. She had to show Greeny that she was in charge.

Besides, what would Mum think if Amelia fell apart at the first sign of trouble? She would know Amelia really wasn't prepared to go on missions.

"Their suits probably just aren't working right," Amelia said finally. "Or they've been brought onto a ship, and the hull is blocking their life signals. Even a big piece of debris could block the signals."

The two young crew members stood silently for a long moment. They just watched the screen. There were still only the three white dots.

"Or they're dead," Greeny whispered.

That was possible too, but Amelia didn't want to admit it.

"They're not dead," she said. She hurried to the weapons locker and pulled out a stun ray. "They'll be back, Greeny. Until then, we hide in the basement."

Greeny shook his head.

"Come on, it'll be fine," Amelia said, taking his wrist. "You know it's safe."

"Uh-uh," Greeny said. "It's not safe now. We opened the basement, remember? Don't *you* know what happens to living things in space? They can't breathe. They freeze. They die."

"Oh, right," Amelia said. "I'll close the doors and repressurize."

She slid her finger across the control panel's touch display. They heard the grind of the doors closing.

Thunk!

The grinding stopped.

The ship suddenly dipped hard to the side. Amelia screamed and grabbed onto the panels.

Greeny didn't react so quickly. He slid across the bridge and slammed into the navigation panel. "Ugh!" he cried.

Amelia rushed over. Greeny held his left arm with the other and yelped in pain.

"What was that?" he asked in a high whine.

"I don't know," Amelia said.

The control screen started flashing red.
A screeching alarm sounded all around them.

Greeny covered his ears and whined louder.

"Warning! Warning!" said a robotic voice.
"Cargo doors failing to close. Error A16-R. Please
reboot ship's central computer. Warning! Warning!
Cargo doors failing to close. Error A16-R . . ."

"All right, all right!" Amelia said. "How do
I re–"

"Intruder alert!" the voice said. Somehow it
sounded even more urgent. "Unknown life forms
in lower cargo bay. Intruder alert!"

6

"Intruders?" Greeny shouted. "It's the aliens who killed Yaz and McCarthy!"

"Calm down!" Amelia said. "They're not dead. They can't be!"

Greeny curled up against the navigation panel. He was shaking, and the air filled with that musky smell of fear.

"You have to call Captain Fist! Before the aliens get us too!" Greeny howled.

"The intruder alert is probably just part of that error A16 or whatever. . . ," Amelia said. "Besides, the captain can't bring the *Meddler* in this close to a debris field. We have to work this–"

The warning repeated. The shrieking alarm squealed and screamed. Greeny howled louder and louder.

Amelia ran back to the main controls. She poked at everything on the display she could think of, but nothing changed.

Finally she slammed her fist down on the screen.

Everything stopped. The error report, the intruder alert and the screeching alarm all went silent. Even the ship itself seemed to grow quiet. Its usual mechanical hum became more like a whisper.

Amelia sighed. "See?" she said. "Everything is fine now."

But the silence didn't last. From below came the loud thud of boots on the metal floor of the basement.

Greeny's ears perked up. His eyes went wide.

"It's Yaz and McCarthy," Amelia whispered. "It has to be."

Greeny sniffed the air. He shook his head. His pointy ears bent back and went flat.

Amelia looked at the stun ray in her hand. She wasn't ready for a blaster fight.

"We have to hide," she said, looking quickly around the room.

The thumping footsteps slowed and stopped beneath the basement hatch.

Greeny snarled at the floor.

"The suit storage," Amelia hissed. With Yaz's and McCarthy's suits gone, there would be room for Amelia and Greeny to squeeze inside.

She grabbed Greeny by the wrist and pulled him to the locker of spacesuits. Greeny snarled and snapped.

"*Shhh!*" Amelia said and closed the doors.

The locker was unlit when the doors were closed. It'd be hard to spot them among the suits. But the locker was airtight. Before long they'd run out of air to breathe. If that wasn't Yaz and McCarthy coming aboard, they'd be in trouble.

"Quick, put a suit on," Amelia said. She started climbing into the smallest one. She slipped her e-pad into the suit's pocket. "We'll be able to hide in here a while with the extra oxygen in the suit tanks."

A low growl rumbled deep inside Greeny's chest, but he obeyed. As he tried to push his injured arm into the suit, he let out a whimper. Amelia quickly helped him pull it on the rest of the way.

"And be quiet," Amelia whispered. "Do you want them to hear us?"

Amelia clicked on her helmet. She watched through the locker door's glass panel as the hatch in the floor popped up.

A pair of hands in thick gloves grabbed the rim of the opening.

Greeny's growl grew louder.

A helmet rose up from the hatch, and then a body in a spacesuit. The suit was such a dark green that it almost looked black. The helmet completely hid the owner's face.

Every crew member of the *Meddler* wore an orange spacesuit with a fist symbol painted on the chest. That wasn't Yaz, and it wasn't McCarthy.

This was an alien. And it wasn't alone.

Two more climbed through the hatch and closed it. Two of the aliens wore plain green suits. The third's suit was marked with three gold stripes on each shoulder.

None of them took off their helmets as they walked onto the bridge. They were probably unsure whether the air on the *Saber* was safe.

"There's no one else here, Commander," said one. His voice was rough. "Our spy must have been wrong."

Spy? Amelia thought. *Someone aboard the* Meddler *is working with these aliens?*

Amelia couldn't believe it. No one would betray the *Meddler* crew.

The commander grunted. He went to the control panel and swiped the display. "This has been used since the two humans left the ship," he said. "Someone else is aboard."

He turned back towards his officers. "See?" he snarled. "I have faith in my spy. Now *find the others!*"

The commander sat down in the pilot seat. The other two aliens moved slowly through the small ship.

Amelia held her breath. It wouldn't take them long to discover her and Greeny.

"Now what?" Greeny whispered desperately.

Amelia's brain reeled.

"We're trapped," Greeny said. He started whining from deep in his throat. "We should tell them we're here. Maybe they won't hurt us."

But Amelia refused to accept it.

She watched the aliens. They tapped the floor panels with their boots, looking for secret doors. One opened the locker of first-aid supplies. He stomped on the contents with one huge boot.

The other ripped off the navigation panel. The wires crackled and snapped, sending sparks flying.

"Look what you've done, fool!" the commander said. "That was the navigation system. We might need that for our mission!"

"Sorry, sir," the alien said. He struggled to put the panel back, but it barely stayed in place. The lights flickered weakly on the broken panel.

"Lights," Amelia whispered to herself.

"What?" Greeny said.

Amelia looked up. Three small lights were set into the ceiling of the locker they were hiding in.

And where there were lights, there were wires. That meant there had to be some space above the locker.

"Can you get that panel off?" Amelia asked, nodding towards the lights above them.

She linked her fingers to make a boost for Greeny. He whined a bit and glanced outside.

"Get moving, Cabin Boy. That's an order," Amelia hissed.

Greeny turned back and climbed up. He got to work with the sharp claws on the hand of his uninjured arm.

The aliens moved closer to their hiding place. One opened the weapons locker, just to the right of them. The alien pulled out two stun rays and a pair of electro-pulsers. He dumped them in the middle of the floor.

"No one in here," he grunted.

"Hurry, Greeny!" Amelia whispered.

The other alien popped off the top of a box. He tipped it over, and packets of food and water bottles spilled out.

"Got it!" Greeny said as the panel came loose. He slid it into the open space above.

"Now get up there!" Amelia said.

Greeny vanished into the darkness.

The two aliens stopped in front of the spacesuit locker.

Amelia gasped. She looked up. "Greeny!"

One of the aliens tugged at the door. The latch was stuck.

He tugged harder.

"Greeny!" Amelia snapped, and so did the latch as it broke and fell off.

Suddenly a hairy hand came down from the opening above. Amelia grabbed it, and Greeny pulled her up into the tiny crawl space. It was crowded with wires and plastic tubing – and now a human girl and a dog-boy.

Amelia hurried to slide the cover back in place just as the locker doors were flung open. She held her breath. She could hear the alien searching through the suits.

After a few moments, the shuffling stopped. "Nothing here," the alien said.

With a sigh, Amelia slumped against the metal wall. "That was too close," she whispered.

Greeny nodded, panting. She could barely see him in the low light. But his big, wet eyes shined. So did his sharp teeth, covered in spittle.

Amelia looked around. They couldn't hide in the crawl space forever. They couldn't fight off the intruders. They were running out of options.

"We have to get a signal to the *Meddler*," Amelia told Greeny. She remembered her study sessions with Yaz. "Maybe we can reach the back of the navigation panel from here. It has communication functions. We could use it to send a message."

"Yes," Greeny said. "Get Captain Lightheart. Get her here."

"OK. I'll go to the nav panel," Amelia said. She tried to sound calm. "Stay put."

She crawled through the narrow tubing. It was much smaller than the air system tubes on the *Meddler*. Amelia moved by squirming like a snake. She stretched her arms out in front. Her leg muscles cramped.

She was sure every scrape of her spacesuit against the metal was echoing through the ship. At any moment, she expected blaster fire to pierce the tube. That would be the end of her first – and only – adventure away from her ship.

And from her mother.

"If I get out of this," Amelia whispered to herself, "I promise to never disobey a direct order from the captain again. Or from my mum."

But the blaster shots never came. In fact, besides Amelia's shuffling and heavy breathing, the tubing was completely silent. She couldn't even pick up Greeny's panting.

Amelia tried to glance over her shoulder, but the tube was too tight. She couldn't look back.

What if the aliens had found and snagged Greeny? What would they do to him if they did?

She couldn't think about that now. The only way to save him and herself was to get a message to Mum on the *Meddler*. Amelia kept squirming forwards until she reached the navigation panel.

The back of the nav panel was the largest section of wiring on the *Saber*. It controlled the ship's autopilot, which was a very complex system. The autopilot included communication controls, the galactic positioning systems and the main navigation computer. Sending an emergency signal from it should be easy.

But it wasn't going to be easy today. Amelia could see that immediately. She had reached the nav panel, but it was hopeless.

When the alien had torn off the nav panel to search for the stowaways, he had also torn most of the wiring. Almost no connections remained.

If Yaz had been with her, maybe *she'd* be able to fix the wires enough to get a message out. But Yaz wasn't here. Yaz was almost certainly dead, and Amelia was definitely lost.

Amelia looked back through the tubing. She hadn't gone far, even though it felt as if it had taken an eternity.

"Greeny!" she whispered into the darkness.

The dog-boy didn't reply.

"Can you fix this mess?" she asked.

Still no reply.

Why can't he hear me? she thought, frustrated. She began to crawl back to report the damage.

But she stopped halfway when she spotted a glint of cold light. It was coming off a green helmet sticking up into the tubing.

It's an alien! Amelia thought. *They've found the panel in the locker and taken Greeny. If I can't get in touch with the* Meddler, *they'll do to Greeny whatever they've done to Yaz and McCarthy.*

Amelia gulped. *And then they'll get me.*

"She's up here," said a rough voice.

"Well, grab her!" replied the commander's mean voice.

Amelia was out of time. She had to try something, and she needed to do it soon.

She started wriggling backwards as the alien came all the way up into the small space. Then she felt something dig into her leg. It was her e-pad.

Amelia's mind raced. The e-pad could send out an emergency signal. But it wouldn't be anywhere near as strong as one from the *Saber*. It wouldn't reach the *Meddler*. She needed something to boost the e-pad's signal.

"The debris," she whispered to herself. "There was a nav panel out there. It wasn't busted up."

If Amelia could find the other nav panel, she might be able to power it up with her e-pad. The nav panel might strengthen the e-pad's signal. And then the message might reach Mum on the *Meddler*.

At least it was a better plan than getting captured.

Amelia pushed on. She did her best to ignore the alien trying to shove his way through the tubing. He growled as his bulky suit clanged against the metal.

For once, her small size was an advantage.

The tube ended. Looking through a vent, Amelia could see she had reached the *Saber*'s front window. To the side of it, she could see a narrow red handle. It was the window's emergency release.

Amelia quickly double-checked the locks on her spacesuit's helmet. "I hope this works," she mumbled.

In one swift motion, she knocked out the vent cover, jumped down, and grabbed the red handle. She pulled.

The window popped loose and flew out into the debris field. All the ship's oxygen rushed out through the opening.

And Amelia and the aliens went with it.

8

Amelia spun wildly out into space.

Swirls of colour filled her vision. She could spot the huge orange planet below. Broken ship parts sparkled all around her.

Amelia tried to keep her breathing calm even as she twirled. She knew she needed to save her suit's air, and panicking would only use more of it.

She grabbed onto a huge chunk of metal to steady herself. It slowed her spin.

"My first spacewalk," Amelia muttered. Her voice sounded strangely flat inside the helmet. It made her feel lonely. "Definitely not how I imagined it."

She quickly looked around. She spotted three green alien spacesuits tumbling through the debris. There wasn't any sign of an orange *Meddler* spacesuit – no Greeny. Maybe he'd been taken to the aliens' ship. She hoped he was OK.

Amelia pushed those thoughts away and focused on her mission. She scanned the scrap floating by. A hundred metres away, she saw it.

The large nav panel. It was still in perfect condition, just as she remembered. A few bursts of air from the oxygen tank on her back would push her towards it.

But the three aliens had stopped spinning. They turned towards Amelia.

Two dived for her. Their huge green suits moved smoothly through the debris field. They dodged and weaved among the wreckage.

Amelia used two puffs of her air to slide along a wide metal pipe. It was just big enough for her to hide inside. She dragged her feet in and pushed her hands against the tube, holding herself there.

It was dark inside. Amelia looked out of the end she'd come in. A green suit silently glided past.

The alien didn't see her.

Slowly, she moved herself back to the pipe's opening. She spotted the two aliens not far off. They both had blasters charged and ready. They were hunting through the wreckage.

Amelia checked her oxygen levels. The display said it was at thirty-six per cent.

She risked one shot of air to thrust herself towards the floating nav panel. It was closer now, and Amelia drifted right towards it.

Someone grabbed her foot. *The third alien!* she thought.

She stopped a few metres short of the nav panel. Her breath caught in her throat. She tried to turn her head, but the spacesuit was too bulky for her to get a good look at her attacker.

Amelia kicked and struggled. She couldn't break loose. She had no choice. She needed to use the last of her suit's oxygen to blast herself away.

Amelia pressed her finger down on the thrust button of the suit's controls. Still the alien held tight. She felt as if her foot might come clean off as more oxygen gushed out of her suit, pushing harder and harder.

Then suddenly she was free.

She heard the tear of fabric as she pulled away. She felt a leak near her ankle. A sharp *ding* sounded in her ear. It was the emergency life-support system kicking in. She'd be out of oxygen soon.

As Amelia glided the last couple of metres to the nav panel, she looked back. She expected to see an alien reaching for her, but she didn't.

Instead she saw a scrap of fabric. It was stuck on the sharp edge of a huge piece of metal.

It hadn't been an alien at all. She'd just snagged her suit on the debris.

At the nav panel, Amelia quickly pulled her e-pad from her suit pocket. She connected it to the nav panel. After tapping the e-pad's screen, she waited for the emergency signal app to open.

"Come on, come on," she told the little computer.

BEEP! BEEP! BEEP!

The suit blared angrily at her. "Warning," said a robotic voice. "Nearing dangerously low levels of oxygen. Return to your ship at once."

"I don't have a ship to return to," Amelia said. "Except the *Meddler*, and if I make it back there, I'll probably never leave it again."

The emergency signal app opened. It would send a message to the *Meddler* faster than the speed of light. Mum would know where Amelia was and that she was in big trouble.

If it worked.

Amelia tapped the red circle in the corner. A message in large letters flashed across the screen: SIGNAL SENT.

If it didn't work . . . well, Amelia couldn't think about that.

She began to feel light-headed.

She was running out of air.

Amelia was in a debris field in a star system in the middle of nowhere, without her mum, without her family aboard the *Meddler*. Even without Greeny.

Something grabbed her ankle. This time, Amelia looked down and saw at once that it was no snag.

"Warning," said the robotic voice in her ears. "Only thirty seconds' worth of oxygen remains. Return to your ship at once."

The alien's grip around her ankle was like a vice. Amelia's vision swam. Her breathing was short and weak. She felt cold.

The alien snarled and tugged at her leg. Amelia was pulled backwards. She hit her helmet against the nav panel, knocking her e-pad loose. She watched the e-pad spin off to join the rest of the debris.

Then everything went black.

9

Amelia slowly opened her eyes. She was on a hard, narrow bed. It felt sort of like the one in her private quarters, except here it was dark and cold. The air smelled strangely familiar.

Was she back on the *Meddler*?

She had sent the emergency signal, hadn't she? Had Mum seen it?

Had she been rescued?

"She's waking up," said a familiar voice.

"Greeny, is that you?" Amelia asked. She could barely speak.

"Don't sit up yet," Greeny said. "You've been out for a long time."

Amelia almost cried in relief. Then they really *had* been rescued.

"Where am I?" she said. "The medical bay? Did Mum come?"

"You're . . . safe," Greeny replied. His voice sounded different.

"What about Yaz?" Amelia said. She struggled to lift her head, but it hurt so much to try. "McCarthy?"

"You'll see them soon," Greeny said. "Relax."

She heard his toenails scratch against the metal floor. "You're not hurt?" she asked.

"Me?" Greeny said. "Nah. Just a bruised arm. Besides, it was worth it. I'll probably be promoted."

"Promoted?" Amelia said. "What are you talking about? My mum is going to kill us both."

Greeny laughed in that barky way of his.

"Why are you laughing?" Amelia said. She sat up, even though it was painful.

It was so dark that she could see almost nothing around her. The bed sat in a small room. She could just make out Greeny's outline in the darkness.

"Where are we?" she said, and suddenly a bright beam of light shined on her face.

She squinted and tried to see who else was there. "Greeny, where are we?" she asked again.

Her blood went cold. The hairs on her arms stood up. She sniffed the air. It was so familiar.

She recognized it now. It was like Greeny's smell but a hundred times stronger – and a hundred times worse.

"You have been captured, pirate girl," said a different voice. It was deep and growly. "By the Canus Anti-Piracy Police Force."

"Canus . . . ," Amelia said to herself.

She thought back to the *Meddler*'s attack on those two outer moons, when the CAPF had let them slip away. She remembered how fierce the security guards were.

She could picture their sharp teeth, hungry for blood. And those guards had been untrained. These officers – the officers of the CAPF – would be more skilled and every bit as rabid.

And here she was, captured. Her skin crawled as she imagined what they might do to her.

Then she remembered Greeny. He was a citizen of Canus. But he was also her crewmate, her partner on this mission. Her friend.

"Greeny!" she shouted.

She rose from her bed. Her weak legs barely carried her, but she hobbled towards the small figure across the metal floor.

"These are your people!" she said. "Can't you tell them we were just collecting scrap, that we meant no h—"

But Amelia never reached him. Instead she walked right into a clear, thick plastic wall and fell backwards. She pressed her hands to her aching head. She groaned.

"Greeny," she said, "you're working with them? You . . . you were the spy the commander mentioned!"

"That's me," Greeny said. "The smelly spy. And that commander is my father."

Amelia heard the wet, hot sniff of his breath through the walls of her plastic cage.

"You see, I didn't really stow away," Greeny said. "I went undercover. We knew how easily fooled your species is by – what do you call them? 'Puppy dog eyes'?"

Canine voices echoed with a howlish laugh.

"You fell right into our trap," Greeny finished. "It was almost too easy."

"You caught me," Amelia said. "And Yaz and McCarthy too?"

"Correct," said the commander's deep voice.

"So this whole thing was just a trick to capture three crew members of the *Meddler*?" Amelia said.

"The *Meddler*," the commander said, "has been a thorn in the side of Canus and our allies for too long. Piracy is not tolerated in our system."

Amelia saw the commander now. He stood next to Greeny. The bright light shined from behind his head. He wasn't wearing a helmet any longer, and she could see the outline of his dog-like features.

She felt the Canus officers circling her plastic cell. Like wolves getting ready to go in for the kill.

But inside Amelia felt a piece of her mother – the bravest captain in the galaxy – grow in her heart.

"So you've got me and two low-ranking officers," Amelia said. She heard her mother's voice in her own. "But you'll never catch the *Meddler*. It's probably a million light years away by now. That means the *real* pirate threat has slipped through your fingers again, just like on Canus."

"Is that right?" said the commander. Amelia could hear angry disappointment in his voice.

"Yep," Amelia said. She went back to her bed and sat on its edge. She tried to be confident and calm, like her mother would have been – like Fist would have been. "You've failed your mission."

The commander moved closer. She could see him clearly now. He had a long snout and yellowish fangs that were wet with saliva. His narrow, brown eyes stared at her as if she was a raw bone with scraps of flesh clinging to it.

"But won't Captain Lightheart come here to Canus to save her daughter?" the commander asked, and he grinned. He had a toothy smile, just like his son. But on Greeny it looked friendly, even funny. On the commander it was sinister and cruel. "After all, you pulled that neat little trick of sending an emergency signal from your e-pad."

Amelia had forgotten about that. If the signal had gone through, Mum would probably be on her way right now.

"Of course she'll save me," Amelia said. She sat up straighter. "The *Meddler* has been to Canus before, and we took what we wanted. What's one little prison break?"

The commander frowned, and Amelia smiled with pride. She was strong in the face of danger. She was brave and tough. She was everything her mother was, and everything her mum wanted her to be.

Sitting there all alone in her plastic cell, Amelia *truly* felt like Little Fist for the first time in her life.

"I see," the commander said. His voice was deep with worry.

Greeny stepped over, into the light. The former cabin boy was wearing an official Canus Anti-Piracy Police Force uniform. He looked up at his father and whined.

The commander looked back with wide eyes. Amelia knew they were both terrified because Captain Fist would be coming for them.

They had stolen away the legendary pirate's daughter and her ship. Captain Fist would make them pay.

The commander stood tall and lifted his chin. "Lights!" he snapped.

Somewhere one of the Canus prison workers heard the barked command. The full lights started to flicker on.

Amelia blinked. She looked around her in a daze.

Her plastic cage was not very big, and it wasn't alone in this prison. More filthy prison cells with thick, see-through walls lined the corridor. They were stacked like boxes of cargo, and they went on for as far as she could see.

Opposite her were Yaz on one side, and McCarthy on the other. But what made her heart sink into the pit of her gut, and what made her skin crawl, was beyond them.

As the lights came up, she saw First Mate Sen. She saw Dr Pectin. She saw Kriley and Jerrette from engineering.

The entire crew of the *Meddler* was here.

That meant–

"Mum!" Amelia shouted, slamming her fists against the plastic wall.

Captain Lightheart jumped up in her cell and pounded against the wall. Mum was screaming back, but Amelia heard nothing. The cells were soundproof.

Amelia could see her, but she couldn't reach her.

The commander stepped even closer to the wall of Amelia's cage. He leaned forward and pushed a mic button on his uniform. The speaker in the cell crackled.

"Who, little pirate," the commander teased, "will save you now?"

SPACE JUNK

The debris field that the *Saber* investigates is not unique in the universe. According to NASA, Earth is surrounded by millions of pieces of orbiting space junk! This includes old satellites that have stopped working, boosters that fell away from travelling rockets, or bits of spacecraft that have broken off.

Many of these pieces are smaller than a marble. But over 20,000 are the size of a tennis ball or larger. That could cause a lot of damage to a floating astronaut!

Space debris circles around planets at thousands of kilometres per hour. In order to safely check out any valuable items, the *Saber* would need to orbit the orange planet at roughly the same speed as its debris. If the astronauts and the space junk are moving at different speeds, the debris might zoom past Officer Yaz. Or a small, marble-sized chunk might rip through her helmet!

Not all space debris floats. Humans have left more than 180,000 kilograms of junk on Earth's Moon. But Captain Lightheart probably wouldn't consider every piece of it valuable. The lunar rubbish includes plastic bags of astronauts' urine! Think about that next time you look up at our shiny, white Moon.

GLOSSARY

bridge control centre of a ship

cargo objects carried by a ship

debris pieces of something that has been broken
or destroyed

depressurize release pressure of a gas (such as air) from
inside a closed space

ensign lowest-ranking officer in some military groups

intruder person who goes into an area where he or she
isn't allowed

navigation processes and systems that move a ship
from one place to another

scrap old material, such as metal, that can be broken
down and used again in some other way

stowaway person who hides on a ship in order to travel
without being seen